# once in a blue moon

## Magnus Mills

This edition published in the UK by
**acorn book company**
PO Box 191
Tadworth
Surrey KT20 5YQ

**email: info@acornbook.co.uk**

**www.acornbook.co.uk**

ISBN 0-9544959-0-X

British Library Cataloguing in Publication Data.
A catalogue record for this book is available from the British Library.

for Graham

# CONTENTS

once in a blue moon

My mother's house was under siege. One chill Friday evening in November I arrived to find the entire neighbourhood in a state of high alert. The police had blocked the street at both ends. A helicopter was circling overhead, and there were snipers hidden in the garden.

'Get down!' they hissed, when I approached.

'It's OK,' I replied. 'I've been on this case right from the beginning.'

After a couple of routine questions they directed me to the officer in command. He was a harassed-looking individual, sheltering with the rest of his men behind an armoured car. The guys were at a complete loss as to what to do next. They stood around, drinking coffee from paper cups, and waiting for something to happen. When I joined them I received no more than a cursory glance.

'Would you like me to talk to her?' I offered.

'Be my guest,' said the chief. 'When all this is over I'm handing in my badge. After that I'll be back on traffic duties. For good.'

He got on his radio and ordered the helicopter to move away. Then I ducked beneath a chequered tape bearing the words POLICE LINE: DO NOT CROSS.

To tell the truth I had scant idea what to expect. It was a while since I'd last called on my mother, having been fully occupied with work and so forth. The usual story. There was no excuse for my neglect, and as I crossed the garden towards the darkened dwelling I felt more than a little uneasy. A heavy silence lay about the place. The only disturbance was the humming of the power generators somewhere behind me. In the cold autumn air I could feel the heat of the searchlights on the back of my neck. There was nowhere to hide.

The commander had given me a loud-hailer. Now I raised it to my lips, spoke into the mouthpiece, and heard a staccato voice ricochet through the night.

'Alright mother!' it rasped. 'I'm going to count to three, and then I want you to come outside with your hands held high above your head.'

I lowered the loud-hailer and waited. From the

house there came not a sound. Its blank windows seemed to stare down at me as I stood all alone in my mother's garden. I tried again.

'Can you here me, mother?!'

To the rear of me I could sense growing restlessness. I knew it wouldn't be too long before the police became impatient and began to resort to less subtle methods. This was my last chance.

'Mother?'

The quiet was shattered as an upper window exploded into smithereens. Then the barrel of a gun appeared, and behind it, my mother's face.

'Whaddyawant?!' she hollered.

It was a good question, and I realised I needed to think carefully before I answered. What I really wanted, of course, was to be able to converse with my mother as I had done in the past. Countless were the times when the two of us had sat in her living room, exchanging remarks about the weather while we shared tea and buns. The clock on the shelf would tick resolutely round for half an hour or so, and then I'd take my leave and all would be well. Her tone this evening, however, suggested that circumstances had changed. I was in danger of being viewed as a representative of the besieging forces. Therefore I required an angle.

'We were wondering,' I said, addressing her once more through the loud-hailer. 'We were wondering what you were doing at Christmas?'

'Who wants to know?' she demanded.

'Just about everybody,' I replied.

A blaze of gunfire told me my mother was in no mood for quips. Nonetheless, as the noise faded away, she offered what seemed like an olive branch.

'You can come in for a few minutes,' she announced. 'But make sure there's no funny business.'

An instant later she'd withdrawn the gun and vanished from sight.

'I'm going in,' I called back to the police chief. 'Wish me luck.'

'You'll need it,' came his answer as I headed for the front door. To my surprise it was off the latch, swinging open at the lightest touch. I stepped into the gloom of the hallway and was grabbed roughly from behind. Then I was frisked for weapons before being led inside.

'Sit there,' said my mother, indicating a hard wooden chair. 'And I'll go and put the kettle on.'

I did as I was told. My seat was not comfortable, but I thought it would be unwise to comment on the fact. From the kitchen I heard reassuring domestic noises. Meanwhile, I glanced around the room I was in. It had been stripped of all but the barest necessities. On the table lay a large pile of used bank notes. I was still gazing at them when my mother came back.

'You planning on doing some wallpapering?' I enquired.

She levelled the gun at me.

'If you know what's good for you, you'll cut the crap.'

'Alright,' I said. 'Sorry.'

'Now what's all this about Christmas?'

'The thing is,' I answered. 'We thought you might like to come to us this year.'

'Why should I?'

'Because you deserve a break.'

'I don't know why you're so concerned all of a sudden,' she said. 'You only call on me once in a blue moon.'

'And how often do you call on me?' I countered.

'As often as not,' she replied.

'Well then.'

'Well then nothing.'

Her new-found bluntness left me lost for words, and there followed an awkward hiatus in our conversation. Fortunately, I was saved by the kettle, its forlorn whistle calling away my reticent host. While she was gone I went to the window and peered through the slats of the blind. I saw immediately that the security cordon had been withdrawn by some thirty metres, which struck me as a sensible precaution. From this vantage point I could also see the full extent of my mother's scorched earth policy. When I'd crossed her garden a little earlier I'd been too preoccupied to notice the conspicuous absence of plant life. Gone were the neat flower-beds which in previous years would have been full of biennials, recently transferred from the greenhouse. This structure now lay in ruins, while the lawn had become nothing more than a wilderness. Even the line of poplars that ran along the boundary fence had been felled, allowing a fresh breeze to blow in from the west.

When my mother returned she was bearing a fully-laden tea tray.

'Oh,' I said. 'You shouldn't have bothered.'

'I know I shouldn't,' she replied. 'But you don't look as if you'd been fed properly since the last time you were here.'

'Yes, well, I've been busy.'

'So have I.'

Something in her voice made me glance up, and I knew I was soon to discover what this was all about.

'Don't look so startled,' she said. 'I've done nothing illegal.'

'What is it then?' I asked.

She smiled. 'Remember when you said I ought to get out more?'

'Yes?'

'Well, I've been getting out more. A lot more.'

'That's good.'

'And I've realised I've been letting life pass me by for far too long. I saw that all the niceties and the considerate deeds had come to nothing, so I decided to make a few changes. First I went to the bank and took out all my money. There it is on the table. They didn't like giving it back, but they had no choice. Then I closed my accounts at the butcher's, the hairdresser's, and the garden centre. Not much, I know, but it's turned me into a free woman. I owe nobody nothing, and I can do whatever I like, whenever I like.'

'And the gun?'

'The gun's only for ornamental purposes.'

'So it's a replica, is it?'

'No,' she said. 'It's real.'

*

I ate my sandwiches and drank my tea. Then I nodded towards the street outside. 'Looks as if you've been attracting attention. Maybe you need to cool it down a little bit.'

'I know, I know,' my mother conceded. 'The feds haven't got used to me yet, so they tend to drop by from time to time. After a couple of hours they usually lose interest and disperse.' She went to the window and looked out. 'They've stuck around a little longer than usual this evening, but they'll be gone by midnight.'

'And then you'll go to bed will you?'

'Maybe,' she answered. 'Or then again I might go out on patrol.'

I took a deep breath.

'OK,' I said at length. 'If that's what you want to do it's fine by me. I'll try to call round more often. And the invitation for Christmas still stands, of course.'

My mother thought for a moment. 'Tell you what,' she said. 'You can come here this year if you like.'

'Thanks,' I replied. 'If you're sure it won't be too much trouble.'

'I'm quite sure.'

'Alright then.'

I buttoned my coat and prepared to leave.

'Just one thing though,' she added. 'You'll have to bring your own tree.'

# the good cop

The first time he came into the room I thought he had a rather preoccupied look about him. It was as if his mind was fully engaged in trying to solve some formidable problem, one that had been imposed on him by powers beyond his control. He paid no attention to me, although I was the only person present, and instead paced around the floor, moving from one corner to the next, until eventually he arrived back at the door. This he opened, glancing briefly outside before closing it again.

'Alright,' he said, finally breaking his silence. 'I've only got a few minutes, but if we're quick we should be able to get all this settled before he comes back.'

'Before who comes back?' I asked.

Only then did he look directly into my face. I saw that he was a tired, pale man, obviously over-worked, wearing a shirt and tie (no jacket), his blue eyes regarding me through a pair of heavy spectacles. He remained standing for several long moments, then settled down in the chair opposite mine, at the other side of the desk. After removing his glasses, he leant forward and rested his head in his hands.

'You're not going to be difficult, are you?' he sighed.

I said nothing.

'Because if you're going to be difficult it makes

things very difficult for me.' He raised his eyes to meet mine. Without his glasses they seemed weak, and gave him a sad, vulnerable appearance. 'I only came in here to see if I could help matters along, but if you're going to be difficult there's very little I can do. Don't you understand it would all be so much easier if you let me help?'

He continued gazing across at me, his whole face appealing for me to accept his offer.

'Well,' I said. 'What is it you want to do exactly? To help.'

His look brightened. 'I want you to trust me.'

'Why?' I enquired.

After a short pause he replaced his glasses and smiled. 'Because I'm your friend.'

*

The second time he came into the room he winced when the door clicked shut, as if the sharp sound was an intrusion, jarring the senses unnecessarily. Then he crept to the chair opposite mine and sat down, quiet as a mouse.

'Shouts a lot, doesn't he?' he ventured.

I was about to ask, 'Who does?' when he put his finger to his lips and frowned.

'It's alright,' he said. 'There won't be any shouting while I'm here, you can rely on that. Your ears can enjoy a well-earned rest. We'll have a nice gentle talk, just the two of us, and you can tell me all about it.'

I shrugged. 'There isn't much to tell.'

This brought another smile to his face, a broad, open smile of kindness and understanding. 'Yes, I suppose that's how it must seem from where you're sitting. A barrage of questions, questions, and more questions until eventually you feel as if there's nothing left to say. But let me ask you something. Have I asked you any questions?'

'None to speak of, no.'

He held out his hands, palms upwards. 'Well then. Not once have I shouted at you, or criticised you, or demanded to know anything. Like I said before, I simply want you to trust me, to think of me as your friend.' He reached into his pocket and produced a bar of chocolate, which he passed across the desk. 'Here you are. Expect you could do with a bite to eat, couldn't you?'

'Yes, thanks,' I said, unwrapping the chocolate and breaking off a chunk. 'I have been here rather a long time.'

'Three or four hours?'

'At least.'

'That is a long time,' he agreed, puffing his

cheeks out. 'Yes, the waiting must be the worse part. The interminable waiting. Never knowing what's going to happen, and always wondering who'll be the next person to come through that door.'

'I hadn't thought of it like that,' I said. 'To tell the truth.'

'Really?' he asked.

'Really,' I replied.

'Well, I'm sure you will very soon.' He stood up and glanced at his watch. 'Look, I've got to go now, but I'll be back shortly I promise. In the meantime I'd keep that chocolate hidden if I were you.'

*

The third time he came into the room he looked deeply troubled. He was carrying a steaming hot towel, which he tossed to me before going over to the wall and leaning on one elbow, eyes closed, his fingers pressed hard against his brow. He maintained this stance for well over a minute. Meanwhile, I made full use of the towel, running it over my face and head, and breathing deeply as the vapours entered my pores. When at last he spoke, his voice was grave.

'I'm dreadfully sorry about this, dreadfully, dreadfully sorry. That man can be such a beast at times. A monster. Nonetheless, you must understand that he's only doing his...'

All of a sudden he broke off, and I looked up to see that he was staring at me with a startled expression on his face. He came forward and gave me a closer look, then slumped down in the chair opposite mine.

'Are you alright?' he asked.

'Never better.'

'Not feeling rough?'

'No, not at all.'

'Well then you'd better let me have the towel back. I'm afraid everything has to be accounted for these days. You know how things are. Nice and refreshing, was it?'

'Yes, thanks,' I replied. 'A great comfort.'

My words seemed to perk him up again, because he quickly rose to his feet and walked around the room saying, 'Good, good. A great comfort. That's very good.'

Then he halted in his tracks and turned to face me again. 'The trouble is that it's likely to get worse.'

'Is it?'

'Oh, yes, much, much worse. And of course there'll be little I can do about it because I won't be here to speak up for you.'

'But I thought you said you were going to help.'

'Well…yes,' he stammered. 'I am going to help you, yes I am. But I can only do that…'

'When you come back,' I interrupted.

'Er…yes, that's quite right. I can only help you when I come back.'

\*

The fourth time he entered the room he was sweating profusely. His shirt was unbuttoned at the collar and his tie had come loose. Under his arm he carried a sheaf of papers, which he hurriedly laid out on the desk, glancing at me from time to time and adjusting his glasses when they slipped down his nose.

'Dear oh dear,' he said, breathing heavily. 'Looks like we have an administrative problem. Can you remember what time you were brought in?'

'I wasn't brought in,' I replied. 'I came of my own accord.'

'What!' he said, plainly taken aback. 'Whatever possessed you to do such a thing?'

'I thought it was the best course of action under the circumstances.'

He put his hand to his head and began pacing round in an agitated manner.

'Have you any idea what goes on here?' he demanded. 'In this very room?'

'Well,' I answered. 'Nothing most of the time, from what I've seen.'

'Nothing!? Nothing!? How can you say that after what you've been through? Hour after hour of interrogation, verbal abuse and the ever-present threat of physical violence, and you call that nothing!!'

'But there's only been you here,' I said. 'And you were kind enough to give me a bar of chocolate.'

He stood stock still, stared at me for several seconds, then marched out of the room.

*

When he came back I noticed he had changed his shirt. The new one was ironed, crisp and white, and his tie was knotted perfectly at the centre of his collar. He was also wearing a stiffly-pressed jacket.

'Sorry about all that earlier,' he said, taking the seat opposite mine. 'Staff shortages.'

'Thought so,' I said. 'You're the good cop,

aren't you?'

To my surprise he reached over and slapped me hard across the face.

'Silence!' he barked. 'We will ask the questions!'

they drive by night

It was getting late, very late, and I was getting nowhere. In complete darkness, with the threat of rain moving rapidly in from the west, I peered along the road, hoping that at any moment a suitable pair of headlights would come into view. Two minutes passed. Nothing. There were very few cars on the road this evening, and I hadn't set eye on a van since about half past seven. The occasional vehicles that did go by all seemed to be making local journeys only. They rumbled past in a steady way, their drivers glancing casually at the lone figure standing by the roadside, and then disappeared into the gloom.

'Come on,' I murmured to myself.

This was the worst day's thumbing I'd had for a long while, and it was beginning to get to me. Normally, such a trip would take five or six hours at the most, yet today I'd been on the move since early morning, and still had over a hundred miles to go. If I didn't get a ride very soon I was going to be stuck here for the night. Moreover, it was about to start raining. A gust of wind tore through a clump of nearby trees and rushed across the fields, pursuing a flurry of late autumn leaves. Then, when it faded away, I heard another sound, a faint moan in the distance, as of some great beast labouring under an enormous burden. My ears pricked up, and a moment later a bloom of artificial light appeared between the converging hedgerows. A lorry was coming. There were no street lamps here, so I'd positioned myself near to some reflective posts at the beginning of a lay-by. Hopefully this would help the driver spot me in good time, and give him plenty of opportunity to pull over. As the vehicle approached I saw that it was an eight-wheeler, its load hidden beneath a huge tarpaulin and roped down on all sides. I stuck out my thumb. A whistle of air brakes told me he was stopping, so I grabbed my bag and watched as the lorry veered into the lay-by and came to a juddering halt. Then I ran quickly up to the cab door on the passenger side, where a window was being wound down. A man's head emerged. He was wearing a woolly hat.

'Want a lift?!' he yelled.

He had to yell because of the racket the lorry was making. The whole cab seemed to be shaking with the motion of the engine, which clamoured incessantly beneath the rattling bonnet.

'Yes please!' I yelled back. 'How far are you...?'

'Eh?!' interrupted the man, thrusting his head further out of the window.

'Going south?!' I tried.

'South?!'

I nodded. His head disappeared. Then the door swung open, and I climbed up. To my surprise, the man turned out to be not the driver, but the driver's mate, an occupation I thought had disappeared decades before. He leant back, and with some difficulty I squeezed past him into the middle seat. The driver sat behind the wheel, grinning across me. He too wore a woolly hat.

'Thanks!' I shouted to him above the din. It was

just as noisy inside the cab as outside, or if anything even noisier.

'You in alright?!' he bellowed, jamming the lorry into gear. This involved me moving my right knee out of the way since it was pressed up against the gear stick. I complied, and we pulled away just as some rain began to fall on the windscreen. Second gear required another knee movement, as did third, and not until we got into fourth was I able to relax my leg. The cat's eyes lit up the road ahead and I sat back in my seat, thankful to be moving once more. The noise made by the engine had now risen to a steady drone, augmented by the roar from the exhaust stack, which seemed to be mounted somewhere close behind us.

Because of all this din, I expected conversation within the cab to be kept to a minimum, but after a short while I realised that the driver was speaking to me. I strained to hear him, and managed to catch the end of his sentence.

'...these parts then?!' he wanted to know.

'Just passing through!' I replied. 'I'm on my...'

'You what?!' he bawled, cutting me off. His ears were hidden beneath his woolly hat.

I raised my voice and tried again. 'I'm on my way home for a few weeks!'

'Eh?!' said the man on my left, inclining his head towards me. For the last few moments he'd sat quietly gazing through the windscreen, but now his reverie had been disturbed and he peered at me in an enquiring way.

'I was just telling your friend that I'm on my way home for a few weeks!'

A look of puzzlement crossed his face as he deciphered the words. Then he nodded emphatically. 'Chance would be a fine thing!'

'You what?!' said the driver, leaning across.

'He says, 'Chance would be a fine thing'!' I explained.

'Oh! Yes!' he agreed, after giving the remark some thought. 'Yes! Indeed it would!'

The rain was coming down heavily now. It drummed on the roof and did battle with a pair of very ill-matched windscreen wipers that had been switched on shortly after I came aboard. Each wiper had its own distinct mode of operation. The one on the passenger side swished from left to right with short, vigorous flicks, while the other scraped irregularly back and forth in long, languid strokes which only served to move the rainwater around, instead of actually getting rid of it. In consequence, the driver had a broad though rather dim view of the road ahead, while his mate could see clearly, but only through an extremely narrow segment. It

Magnus Mills

occurred to me that between them their field of vision was probably quite adequate, and I wondered in an idle way if this was the reason they operated as a pair. Certainly they had all the makings of a 'team'. For a start, the two of them were of a very similar appearance, both wearing a donkey jacket as well as the woolly hat I mentioned before. They also had identical accents which placed them as coming from the north-west, although I couldn't say exactly where. Both driver and mate seemed equally bent on pressing forward with the journey, despite such atrocious conditions, their shared concentration evident as they peered intently at the road ahead. When it came to verbal communication, however, there was a problem. The inside of the cab was one of the most deafening places I had ever been, yet my two companions continually tried to discuss our progress, exchanging comments on every bend, puddle or similar hazard we encountered. This would have been alright if either had been prepared to listen to what his partner was saying. Instead, the pair of them constantly interrupted one another with shouts of 'Eh?!' or 'You what?!'

At one point we passed a sign warning of a particularly steep hill ahead, and the driver began the process of selecting low gear, a noisy operation that entailed much revving of the engine and stamping on the clutch pedal. While I deftly adjusted the position of my knee in relation to the gear stick, his mate chose the moment to make a remark about the weather. 'Looks like this rain's…'

' You what?!' yelled the driver.

'Looks like this rain's setting in for the night!!'

From my place in the middle seat I could only just hear what was said. Therefore, I suspected the driver had picked up nothing at all. Nonetheless, I could see that he was about to attempt a reply, so I did my best to lean back out of the way.

'What's getting in?!' he shouted across me.

'Eh?!' replied his mate.

'You said something was getting in!'

''Yes!' came the reply. 'For the whole night I shouldn't wonder!'

They both glanced towards me, apparently to seek my opinion on the matter, so I gave a judgemental nod of agreement, and the pair of them appeared quite satisfied.

Most of the time we had this road completely to ourselves. Occasionally, however, a blurred set of lights would struggle past going the other way, indicating that we weren't the only people trying to travel in this dreadful weather. The rainwater was now practically bouncing off the tarmac, with surges of dense spray being thrown up by our wheels as we ploughed southward through the darkness. After another mile or so, a movement ahead and to the left caught my eye. Twirling round and round in the wind was a revolving sign that marked the entrance to a transport café. On top of it was a metal flap bearing a single word: CLOSED.

Next moment we'd passed it by, and as the deserted roadhouse disappeared behind us, I realised I hadn't eaten for hours. I'd managed to buy a box of individual fruit pies and a carton of milk about four o'clock, but since then I'd had to concentrate so hard on getting a ride that I'd completely forgotten about food. Now my hunger was returning with a vengeance, and I felt a rush of disappointment as it dawned on me that all the cafés were more than likely shut for the night. Fortunately, my two companions were more familiar with this road than I was, and the 'closed' sign triggered off a conversation between them about when and where we were going to stop and eat. This was carried out in the normal way, with many interruptions of 'You what?!' and 'Eh?!', but stuck there in the middle I soon learned quite a lot about our prospects of getting a good meal, or 'bait', as they called it.

Apparently, there was a choice of two places. The first was an establishment known as THE TIGER LILY which, despite its name, had no connection whatsoever with China or Chinese cuisine. This came as a relief as my appetite was veering strongly towards steak-and-kidney pie and chips, rather than noodles. THE TIGER LILY, it seemed, was renowned among lorry drivers (and their mates) as being the place to get a meal quick and cheap at any time of night. It never closed, which was presumably the reason its proprietor, Stanley, never had time to shave, bath, or even wash. My two comrades spent a considerable amount of time swapping jokes about Stanley's bodily hygiene. All the same, they felt a certain bond of loyalty towards the man because they'd known him since before 'the accident'. What exactly had happened wasn't clear, but as I sat listening I began to form a picture of a one-armed (or perhaps one-legged) cook, attempting to manage an all-night café single-handedly, while wearing a heavily-stained apron. Privately, I hoped that THE TIGER LILY would not be our next port of call.

The alternative, I discovered was a commercial restaurant called JOY'S, run by a woman of the same name. This Joy apparently served up the most delicious meals imaginable, in the cleanest possible conditions, but, from what I could gather, ruled her customers with a rod of iron. Most of the drivers on this route were afraid of her. Not only did she make them wipe their feet as they came in through the door, but she forbade anyone from buttering their bread on the table rather than the plate, or from stirring sugar into their tea with the wrong utensil. She was a former beauty queen who'd had several husbands, all of whom were known personally to my two friends, but all of whom were now dead.

'Very harsh woman!' concluded the driver at the end of a long debate. Then he remembered that JOY'S was always closed on Thursday nights when she attended her Highland Dancing Club.

'It'll have to be THE TIGER LILY!' he announced.

After another twenty miles, a glowing light

appeared at the roadside, and a moment later we were turning in. As the lorry's engine fell silent it struck me that these two men would at last be able to hold a conversation without each having to yell at the top of his voice.

Yet ten minutes later, as they sat eating pies, mushrooms, chips and peas, neither of them uttered a single word.

screwtop thompson

'SCREWTOP THOMPSON!' it said on the box. 'HIS HEAD SCREWS RIGHT OFF!' The price was two shillings and sixpence. Screwtop Thompson made his appearance in the toy shop window a few weeks before Christmas, and caught everybody's attention with his jolly laughing face. He came in several different guises. You could buy Screwtop Thompson as a policeman, a fireman, a sailor, a footballer, a boxer or a schoolmaster, each with the same expression. The policeman brandished a truncheon, the fireman held the end of a hose, while the schoolmaster wore a mortarboard and gown.

Screwtop Thompson was plump and round with a big red mouth and shiny black eyes. His head screwed off, apparently so that you could put things inside him – small coins, for example, or maybe your collection of coloured marbles. We were living in an age of austerity, so my parents agreed that Screwtop Thompson would make an ideal Christmas gift for me. I chose the fireman. The price, as I said, was two and six, or half-a-crown, as we called it in those days.

My brother's equivalent present was a robot. It did nothing apart from march along the floor with yellow lights flashing where its ears should be, but at the time it was considered a technological marvel by children and adults alike. There were four sizes in the range, and my brother was to receive the third largest. After the two of us had made our choices, we were supposed to forget we'd ever been in the shop, so that we could be appropriately surprised when we were given our presents on Christmas Day. We did our best but it was difficult. Everybody at school was talking about the new robots and the Screwtop Thompsons, as well as all the other treasures that were arriving in the toy shop day after day. Some of them sounded fantastic.

When I heard about the car-racing kits and the 'genuine walkie-talkies' that were now becoming available, I began to wonder if I'd made the right choice with my Screwtop Thompson. At the same time, I knew it was too late to change my mind.

At last the big day came. On Christmas morning I unwrapped my present and found I had received not a fireman but a schoolmaster. It seemed that there had been such a rush for Screwtop Thompsons in the days preceding Christmas that the shop had run out of all the other lines. I hid my disappointment and reminded myself that even the schoolmaster would have the same jolly face as the rest.

When I removed the lid of the box, however, I discovered that Screwtop Thompson's head was missing. All I had was his body, wrapped in the flowing black gown. This provided a bona fide excuse for tears, and my father had to console me by saying that immediately after the Christmas holiday he would write to the manufacturer to demand an explanation, as well a replacement head.

'We'll have to wait a couple of weeks, though,' he remarked. 'Otherwise the letter will be sure to get lost in the post.'

I stood my Screwtop Thompson on the windowsill and managed to amuse myself with the rest of my gifts. Some of these were edible, of course, and included toffee and chocolate, as well as a number of little sugar mice.

As Christmas Day quickly passed, the batteries in my brother's robot began to run down, so that by teatime it would only move at half speed. Early on he'd discovered that it was altogether hopeless across carpets, and could be used only on a flat, smooth surface such as the hall floor. My mother was worried because our hall was draughty and the weather was turning cold, and I think she was probably quite relieved when, finally, the batteries went completely dead.

As darkness fell, we forgot about toys and instead chose to watch television, the magic of Christmas flashing for hour after hour across a pale-blue screen. Then we went to bed, hoping for all our worth that it would snow overnight.

It was traditional for our cousin Martin to come to stay with us between Christmas and New Year. This was the only time we ever saw him, so we had to renew our acquaintanceship annually. At the beginning of such visits the three of us got on very well together, but relations quite often became strained as the days passed. My mother said that this was because Martin had no brothers and sisters, and was more used to playing on his own than we were. My brother and I therefore received instructions to be nice to him and to make allowances.

There had been no snow as yet, but on the day that Martin arrived the sky had turned very cold and grey, offering prospects of sledging and snowball fights. My brother and I were pleased to find that Martin shared our enthusiasm for these pursuits, and the three of us were soon planning to build an igloo.

In the meantime, we had to exchange gifts. We gave Martin solitaire, and he gave us snakes-and-ladders (which we already had). This meant that sometime after the holidays we would have to write to Martin's parents thanking them and hoping our cousin had got home safely. It also meant we would have to play snakes-and-ladders several times during the next few days. It was while preparations were being made for just such a game that I noticed one of my sugar mice had gone missing.

I'd placed all my presents on one side of the Christmas tree, separate from my brother's, with the sugar mice on top. When I discovered the loss I naturally blamed my brother and a small tussle ensued, during which he denied taking anything. Finally, my father intervened and told me I had probably lost count of how many sugar mice I'd already eaten. This seemed unlikely to me as I had previously divided them into pinks and whites and knew exactly how many there were of each.

Nonetheless, my father commanded me, firmly, to drop the matter.

As all this was going on, Martin sat quietly at the table setting up the board for snakes-and-ladders. Meanwhile, my headless Screwtop Thompson stood unnoticed and forgotten on the windowsill.

My brother and I had a neighbour called Conker, who often called round whether he was invited or not. He lived close by and was about the same age as me, although a good deal larger than any of my other friends. Conker was a rather rough-and-ready companion, and we were more likely to get into trouble if he was with us. He also tended to use his size to administer justice.

I remember one occasion when he saw me shove

my brother into a hedge during a squabble about blackberries. A moment later, he had knocked me to the ground, and he spent the next few minutes sitting on my head singing, ' I will make you fishers of men!' at the top of his voice. As I said, a rather rough-and-ready companion. All the same, we were quite pleased to see him when he turned up one cold morning a couple of days after Martin's arrival.

Martin and Conker had met the year before, and soon we were all talking about our Christmas presents. Conker had also received a Screwtop Thompson. His first choice had been the footballer and, lucky for him, his wish had been granted. The subject of conversation then came round to my own headless version, which Martin suddenly found a source of great amusement. With my brother and Conker as an audience, he took huge delight in mocking me for receiving a model of a schoolmaster for a Christms present, especially one without a head!

He went on to say that he thought all the Screwtop Thompsons were stupid and babyish anyway. I pointed out that they were good for saving up in. Martin said saving up was stupid as well. Conker said this was because Martin's parents probably bought him everything he wanted, so he didn't need to save up. Martin repeated his assertion that Screwtop Thompsons were stupid.

'No, they're not!' I cried, going to the windowsill to get mine. At the same instant we all saw that it was now snowing heavily outside. The argument was forgotten as we rushed about putting on our coats and boots.

My mother appeared and reminded us we needed our bobble hats as well, then the four of us spent the next few hours tumbling around in the growing whiteness. It smothered everything, so that the road and the pavement became indistinguishable under the orange glow of the street lights, which seemed to remain switched on all day (although they most probably weren't).

Before we knew it, evening had come and it was time to get warmed up indoors. We said goodnight to Conker, all of us having decided that tomorrow we would build the igloo we'd talked about.

This was easier said than done. The weather the following day turned out to be cold and harsh, and it had at last stopped snowing: ideal conditions for building an igloo. Unfortunately we were unable to agree the best way to go about it. Conker wanted to make a huge pile of snow and then burrow a way inside, while I preferred the idea of building the igloo properly from snow 'blocks'.

Martin, in the meantime, seemed much more interested in giving orders than anything else. He already had my brother digging snow with a spade that was much too large for him, and he then embarked on an independent scheme to built a giant snowman. He wouldn't let any of us help him, not even my brother, which seemed a bit unfair, so we carried on with the igloo alone. By late afternoon we were starting to wonder how Eskimos could live in such small, cold places. My brother had long since lost interest in the project, and had instead begun to build a snowman of his own, right beside Martin's. Conker and I were emerging from the igloo after a shivering competition when we saw Martin shoving a stick into my brother's snowman's neck. He obviously thought we weren't looking, and didn't seem to care that my brother was standing nearby with a very distraught expression on his face. Martin pushed the stick further and further before levering it back, so that the head was prised off and rolled on to the ground. My brother rushed forward to save his creation, but Martin knocked him to one side. This was too much for Conker, who charged from the igloo towards Martin's snowman, with the obvious intention of destroying it.

At that moment Conker's father appeared at the gate and ordered his son to come home for tea immediately. 'We've been calling you for ten minutes!' he announced, clipping the boy round the ear for good measure.

## screwtop thompson

As we headed back towards our house, my brother in tears and Martin grinning quietly to himself, I noticed Screwtop Thompson, the headless schoolmaster, standing silhouetted in the window, as though he'd been observing the afternoon's events unfold.

The day before New Year was a quiet one. My parents had many things to do, they said, so they were leaving us to our own devices for a couple of hours. We were ordered not to traipse snow into the house if we went outside, and not to help ourselves to cake. Would it be alright for Conker to come round? we asked. Yes, they said, that would be alright. They would be back at teatime.

The snow had by now lost its charm for us, so instead we opted to stay indoors for the day. Martin suggested a game of snakes-and-ladders, to which my brother and I both agreed, and when Conker arrived he offered to make up a foursome. Before play could begin, however, there was a matter to settle. As Martin reached for the dice, Conker knocked him down and pinned him to the floor. Then my brother and I did our very best to screw his head right off.

the End

Also by Magnus Mills:


The Restraint of Beasts

only when the sun shines brightly

All Quiet on the Orient Express

Three To See The King

The Scheme for Full Employment

## The Scheme for Full Employment

'I've been having a look at your daily mileage reports for December. According to this you did sixty-three miles on Wednesday the fourth, sixty-three miles on Thursday the fifth, and on Friday the sixth, one million, twelve thousand and twenty-two miles. Where did you go that day?'

The Scheme for Full Employment
is a wonderfully original fable - and a modern classic
in the making.

Published by Flamingo

All our titles are available direct from

acorn book company
PO Box 191, Tadworth
Surrey KT20 5YQ

**POST FREE IN THE UK**

Cheques payable to acorn book company.
or email your order to sales@acornbook.co.uk

Something else by Magnus Mills...

**The School of Hard Knocks**

'I'm sorry to tell you your parents are dead,' said the headmaster. 'They have been murdered in the most horrific circumstances. Your family home is burnt to cinders and your three siblings are missing. You no longer have any means of support. I must request therefore, that you leave the school at once, since you will be unable to pay your fees. Prior to departure you should complete any outstanding written work and hand it in. You should also make your bed ready for inspection by matron.'

He walked to the door and stood holding it open.

'Well, good luck,' he said. 'And be careful: your parents' killers are still at large.'